The Berenstain Bears
Discover God's Creation

by Stan and Jan Berenstain
with Mike Berenstain

ZONDERVAN.com/
AUTHORTRACKER
follow your favorite authors

ZONDERkidz

Living
Lights™

Said Mama Bear,
"It seems to me,
you cubs watch
much too much TV!"

"Don't turn it off!
It isn't fair!"
"Don't turn it off!
Please, Mama Bear!"

"Watching all that
TV slush
will surely turn
your brains to mush.

"I will not argue.
You have no vote.
I will keep
the TV remote!"

"I beg you, Ma,
on bended knee.
Don't take away
our TV!"

But Ma was firm.
Ma knew her mind.
"No more TV
of any kind!

"There's so much more
to do and see.
God gave you eyes
for more than TV!"

The cubs were stunned.
The cubs were shocked.

Those TV-watching bears
were rocked!

Then Brother had a bright idea.
"Look out the window, Sister Bear.
I see another
world out there."

It was Bear Country,
God's creation.
It was lovelier than
any old TV station.

They opened up
the door a crack.
Now there was
no turning back.

When those TV bears
stepped outside,
their TV eyes
opened wide.

There were such amazing
things to see.
The cubs forgot
that old TV.

There was stuff called grass,
things called trees,

and flying things
called birds and bees.
How did God
think up all these?

And way, way,
away up high,
a big blue thing
called the sky.

The cubs loved all
that God had done,
and knew they were in
for much more fun!

There were other cubs
to run and play with,

and when they got tired—
to sit and stay with.

There were playground things
to climb and slide on,

and other things
to climb and ride on.

There was a thing called weather.
Sometimes it rained.

One day it even
hurricaned!

But then that thing
called sun came out
and spread its warmth
and light about.

Said Brother Bear,
"Who needs TV?"
Said Sister Bear,
"TV? Not me!"

"God's creation,
we have found,
has a better picture
and better sound.

And worlds of wonder
all around!
Thanks, Lord,
   for this world we've found!"

"That thing up there
called the moon
means that we should
go home soon!"

But when the cubs got home,
what did they see?
Their papa looking
at TV.

Maybe Papa didn't know
God's creation was better
than any old show!

"Papa! Too much of
that TV slush
will surely turn
your brain to mush!

Come outside,
and you will see
God's creation is much
better than any old TV!"

The Berenstain Bears
Do Their Best

by Stan and Jan Berenstain
with Mike Berenstain

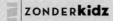
ZONDERVAN.com/
AUTHORTRACKER
follow your favorite authors

ZONDERkidz

Living
Lights™

Look, Sister Bear!
Hooray! Hooray!
The big kite contest
is today!

BIG
KITE
CONTEST
TODAY!

Yes, Brother Bear.
I see. That's right.
But we can't go.
We have no kite!

No kite? No kite?
Now, do not worry.
I can make one
in a hurry!

A kite for me and Sister Bear?
A kite for both of us to share?
Let's thank the Lord from up above
for Papa showing us his love.

I'll make a kite.
Just wait and see,
with the special talents
God gave me!

First some sticks—
just two will do.
Some paper, string,
and a little glue.

We tie.

We cut.

Now, we glue.
See? I made a kite
for you!

A big red kite!
It's a beauty!
Big Red Kite,
do your duty!

It sure is red.
No doubt about it.
But will it fly?
I really doubt it.

For, you see,
without a tail,
that big red kite
is sure to fail.

This old bed sheet
will make a tail.

This tail will help
Big Red to sail.

Kite contest,
we're on our way!
Our big red kite
will win the day!

Kites! Kites!
Up ahead!

Are any as special
as our Big Red?

Kites of every
shape and size
sail and dance
across the skies—

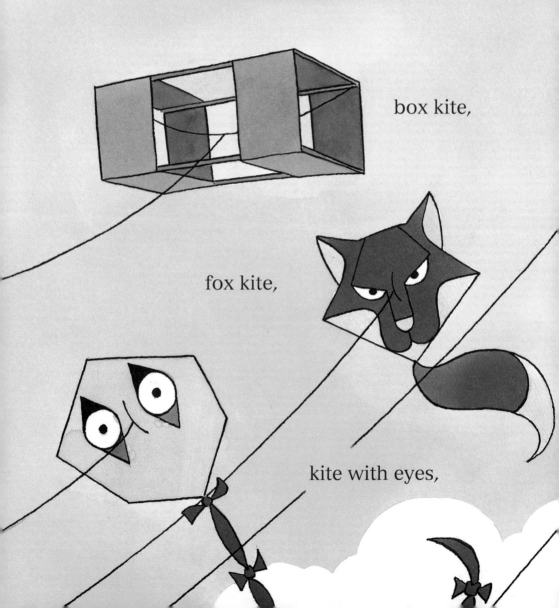

box kite,

fox kite,

kite with eyes,

kites that look like butterflies,

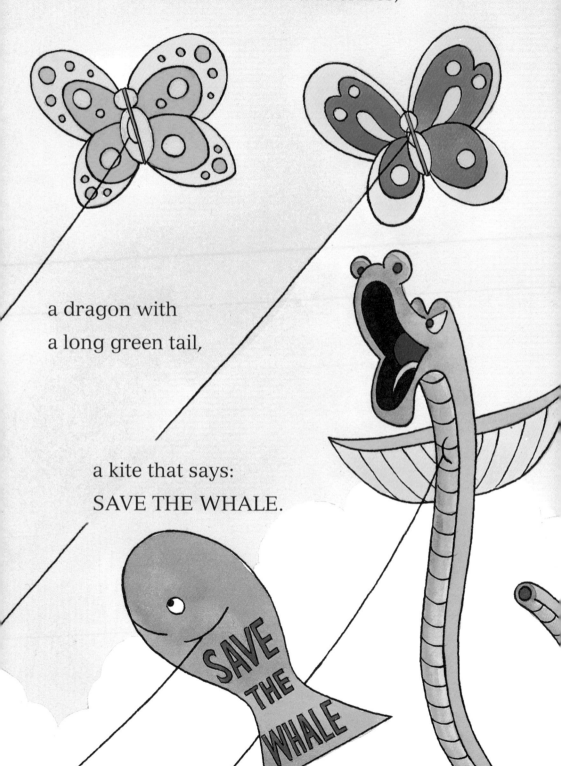

a dragon with
a long green tail,

a kite that says:
SAVE THE WHALE.

The judge looks
down his nose at Red.
"It looks homemade,"
the kite judge said.

Oh? Oh?

Is that so?

It's time to fly?

Here we go!

Run, Papa! Run!
Have faith! Be tough!
But are hope and prayer
going to be enough?

We won't give up!
We'll keep on trying.
Red will soon
be up and flying!

Look, Papa! Look!
The wind grows strong!

In wind like this,
those fancy kites
will not last long!

Look! Red flies high,
and higher still!

I know we'll win!
I know we will!

That wind is strong.
That wind is rough.
Those other kites
weren't strong enough!

But we believed
in Papa's skill.
And our faith in God's help
is stronger still.

Big Red has won
fair and square.
Congratulations,
Papa Bear!

You believed,
you did your best
and that took Red
higher than the rest!

We won! We won,
Mama Bear!

Our big red kite
won fair and square!

You passed a very
important test:
You didn't quit!
You did your best.
Papa, Brother, and Sister,
you are very blessed!

The Berenstain Bears®

Learn to Share

by Stan and Jan Berenstain
with Mike Berenstain

ZONDERVAN.com/
AUTHORTRACKER
follow your favorite authors

 ZONDER**kidz**

Living
Lights™

I'm Sister Bear.
I'm here to say
that what I like
to do is PLAY.

I run.

I skip.

I jump.

I climb.

I have myself
a great old time!

Who's the one
I play with best,
pray and sing with
more than the rest?

Just turn the page
and you will see
my favorite playmate—

little me!

It's lots of fun
to play you see.
I ask my dolls
to come to tea.

I have my games
all to myself,
and every toy
on each big shelf.

But Mama says
almost every day,
"Take time to share.
Take time to pray."

But there are times
I do not care.
My things are mine!
They aren't to share!

I take each turn
on my red truck.

I do not share
my pull-toy duck.

I say inside,
"It's all mine!"
But then I wonder,
is it kind?

Is this the way
that I should be?
A bear that only
thinks of me?

Then I know
it's time to share
my playthings with
my fellow bear.

One is fun,
but it is true
that many games
are best with two.

When I am sure
I need another,
I go look
for my big brother.

We play checkers,

beanbags,

pick-up-sticks.

Spending time with Brother
I get my kicks.

Look! Here come Liz
and Bob and Clem.
Now we can share
with *all* of them.

I ride Bob's bike.
He rides my trike.
It's great. We share
and share alike.

So, sharing's fun.
It's good to do,
and lots of times—
it's easy, too.

And if you share
it's also true
your fellow bear
will share with you!

We share our time
when we're together.
We run, we hide,
skip stones—whatever.

We share our books.

We trade our cards.

We visit one
another's yards.

Now we are more
than three or four.
We're five, six, seven,
and lots, lots more!

Here come Millie,
Mike, and Nat.
Anna May has brought
her cat.

Here comes Fred
with Snuff, his terrier!
This way, friends!
The more the merrier!

Remember Jesus says
that he is with you
when more are together—
like five, four, three,
or two.

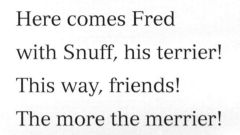

This way, cubs!
Come one! Come all!
We'll choose up sides
to play baseball.

A game of ball
is lots of fun.
We pitch. We bat.
Look! Too-Tall hit
a big home run!

It works out well
if you can share
your playthings
with your fellow bear.

The ball is mine.
It's Freddy's bat.
Lizzy brought
a glove and hat.

She'll share her hat
but not her glove.
Uh-oh! Fred gives her
a little shove.

We all saw
that little shove!
It was not showing
God's care and love.

Soon, there are lots
of arguments.

Of course, I put in
my two cents.

This is not the way.
It's not right!
We should all be sharing,
not in a fight.

And so to keep
the peace between us,
all our friends go home.

"Please think of Jesus.
He would want us to share
and show we love
our fellow bear."

Meanwhile, friends,
it's still today.
And there is still
some time to play.
So turn the page,
and you will see ...

Brother, will you
play with me?